THE GREAT ESCAPE

BOOKS IN THE PUPPY PATROL™ SERIES

COMING SOON

THE GREAT ESCAPE

JENNY DALE

Illustrations by Mick Reid
Cover illustration by Michael Rowe

AN
APPLE
PAPERBACK

SCHOLASTIC INC.
New York Toronto London Auckland Sydney
Mexico City New Delhi Hong Kong

No part of this publication may be reproduced in whole or in part, or stored in a retrieval system, or transmitted in any form, or by any means, electronic, mechanical, photocopying, recording, or otherwise, without written permission of the publisher. For information regarding permission, write to Macmillan Publishers Ltd., 25 Eccleston Place, London SW1W 9NF and Basingstoke.

ISBN 0-439-21811-X

12 11 10 9 8 7 6 5 4 3   1 2 3 4 5 6/0

Printed in the U.S.A.   40
First Scholastic printing, February 2001

SPECIAL THANKS TO TESSA POTTER

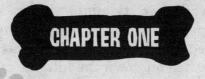

CHAPTER ONE

Neil Parker stopped his bike at the crest of Compton Hill and leaned forward on the handlebars. He cracked a wide, beaming smile toward his sister, Emily, as she pulled up alongside him. "Race you back to King Street Kennels. Last one home has to walk bulldog Biffer for the rest of the week."

Emily steadied her bike, looked across at her brother, and eyed him suspiciously. "Why are you in such a good mood? I thought Mr. Hamley gave you an essay to write yesterday because you made dog noises in his class. You've got no reason to be so cheerful."

"He did — but I don't care! It's the first day of summer vacation, Em, and we've got eight whole weeks to devote to dogs!" Neil and Emily's parents

1

ran a boarding kennel and rescue center for stray dogs. Everybody in Compton knew about King Street Kennels — or the "Puppy Patrol," as their friends called the Parkers. Neil shouted, "C'mon!" and then pushed off down the hill.

As he pedaled furiously to increase his speed, Neil glanced back to see if his sister was catching up. The wind flattened Neil's rough, spiky hair as he put his head down and raced ahead. The kennel was still about a mile away.

Emily was closing the gap between them.

Neil pedaled faster. Soon he'd be out walking in the woods with Sam, his pet Border collie. And he'd be able to help out around the rescue center now that he had so much free time on his hands.

"Watch out, Neil!"

Emily's sudden cry shattered his thoughts.

Something streaked across the road in front of him and into the bushes.

A moment later, there was a screech of tires and the sound of metal crunching. It happened so quickly, Neil could hardly take it all in.

He braked hard. For a second he thought he was going to fly over the handlebars, but miraculously he managed to stay in his seat. He put a foot down to steady himself and tried to stop shaking.

Seconds later, Emily was beside him. "Did you see that?" she yelled, jumping off her bike.

In front of them on the other side of the road, two cars had collided. A large BMW had smashed into the back of a small gray Honda. The drivers were getting out of their cars and didn't seem to be hurt.

Neil noticed that Emily's attention was elsewhere. She wasn't looking at the cars. She was pointing wildly toward the field on their left. "It was a dog! It ran in front of the car. I'm going to see if it's all right."

Emily scrambled down the bank at the roadside. Neil looked back at the cars. A woman was coming toward him. A man was following her, shouting.

"Did you see what happened?" the woman called out. "Is the dog all right? I don't think I hit it." She was small and fair-haired, wearing jeans and a blue jacket. She looked very concerned.

The man was in his early thirties and was dressed in a dark suit. He was tall and thin with a neat mustache. "Would you come back here!" he yelled after the woman. "Look at the damage you've done to my car! You can't just stop like that without signaling."

The woman turned around calmly. "A dog ran in front of me. I had to stop quickly. You were driving too close behind me. You should have been more careful."

"I was about to pass you . . ." he replied.

"On this narrow little road? Just calm down. Our

insurance companies will sort it out. Let's exchange addresses and information."

"You've mangled my bumper and cracked the front end. My headlights are smashed to pieces . . ."

Neil turned away from them. "If everyone is OK, I'm going to help my sister find the dog."

The man glared at Neil. "Yes, the dog! The dog's responsible. What are you doing with a dog loose on the main road? I want your address, too. I've a good mind to call the police right now." He pulled a cell phone from his pocket.

Neil's mouth dropped open in disbelief. "But it's not our dog!"

The woman glared at the man. "It wasn't with them. The animal just shot out from the side of the road. Who knows where the poor creature is now!" She turned back to Neil. "Come on, I'll help you look."

As they climbed down the bank together, Neil could still hear the man yelling. "Just a minute. Come back! We haven't exchanged information yet. I'm late for a meeting."

Neil could see Emily in the far corner of the field. She was kneeling down and keeping very still. Something was lying in front of her on the ground. He suddenly felt his heart racing. Maybe the dog had been injured after all. He hoped Emily was being careful — they both knew that an injured dog might easily bite if it was in pain. He hurried across the newly cut cornfield. He wanted to call out to Emily but he was worried about frightening the dog. He motioned to the woman behind him to keep as quiet as possible.

As they drew closer, Neil heard Emily talking softly to the dog. "It's OK, girl. You're all right now."

The dog was trembling but sitting up. Emily was calmly stroking the dog's short, smooth coat. The hound was a beautiful tricolored beagle, but she looked very grubby. She had a black saddle-shape across her back, edged with soft, tan fur. A white diamond stretched from the dog's muzzle to her fore-

head. The rest of her head was tan, but her legs, chest, and the end of her tail were a dirty white. She was staring up at Emily with gentle, brown eyes.

"I think she's just frightened," whispered Emily. "I don't think she's hurt. She was running around the field, but she stopped when she couldn't get through the bushes. Then she let me come up to her. She's very nervous, though, and look how thin she is."

"Well, done, Em." Neil bent down and put out his hand for the dog to sniff. "Good girl. We'll look after you."

"I hope she doesn't take off again," said Emily, anxiously.

"I think you should stay here while I get help. She obviously trusts you, and we shouldn't risk moving her in case there's something wrong."

The woman knelt down beside them. "Is there anything I can do?" she asked.

Suddenly, they heard shouting. The man was at the bottom of the bank near the roadside waving his arms around to attract their attention.

"He'll scare her if he doesn't quiet down," said Emily.

Neil turned to the woman. "I need to call my dad. We don't live that far away. He'll come get us."

As they hurried back across the field the woman introduced herself. "I'm Wendy Paget. Is your dad a vet?"

Neil shook his head. "No, we live at King Street Kennels. If I can call my dad, he'll know what to do."

"That awful man said something about calling the police. He'll want to report the accident so that he can claim this on his insurance. I'll get him to lend you his cell phone while we exchange addresses."

Wendy Paget seemed to handle the man very well. He was still angry, but he began to calm down as she talked to him.

"This lady tells me your parents run a rescue center for dogs." The man handed his phone to Neil. "I hope it isn't one of their strays. Make your call and get something done about that dog before it causes another accident."

Neil punched in the number. "Hello, Dad? We need your help." Neil could sense the anxious edge to his father's voice and tried to reassure him that nobody was hurt. He quickly filled him in on the situation and finished, "See you in a couple of minutes."

The man grabbed his phone and jumped into the car. "I've really got to rush — I've got an important meeting. My insurance company will be in touch," he snapped. "Good-bye."

Neil and Wendy watched the car maneuver around the other vehicle before speeding away.

"He'll have another accident if he's not careful," said Neil.

Wendy looked at the business card the man had given her. "Well, thanks for your help, Mr. P. Pritchard of Universal Laboratories, Padsham." She turned back to Neil. "I'll wait by the road for your dad. You'd better go back and see if your sister's all right."

"Thanks," said Neil. "You'll have no trouble recognizing him. He'll be driving a green Range Rover with KING STREET KENNELS written on the side."

Bob Parker arrived at the scene shortly afterward and stopped on the grassy roadside. He was a large man with thick, dark hair and a sweatshirt emblazoned with the same puppy logo that was on the vehicle doors.

From the field, Neil heard the car engine and turned to look back at the road. He saw his father and Mrs. Paget up on the bank together. She was pointing in their direction. Moments later, Bob Parker was striding across the field toward them.

"Don't scare her, Dad," called Emily, as he approached them. "She's a bit jumpy."

Bob Parker knelt down and gave the dog a quick once-over. He ran his hands along her back and down each leg, checking for signs of injury. The dog was trembling, but didn't seem to be in any pain. "She's a beautiful dog underneath all this muck, and she's obviously been cared for in the past, but she's very weak and thin. You say she can walk and run OK?"

Neil and Emily nodded. Bob gently slipped a collar on her and attached a leash to it. "You take her, Emily," he said. "Let's bring her back to King Street where we can check her out properly."

Emily stood up stiffly. "Come on, girl."

The beagle responded to Emily's gentle tugs and they walked slowly back toward the road.

"Where do you think she came from, Dad?" Neil asked. "Judging by the dirt on her paws, she must have been lost for some time. She didn't have a collar, either. I wonder why somebody didn't want her."

Bob Parker sighed. "I've given up speculating about things like that, Neil. I've known people to abandon beautiful, good-tempered pedigree dogs for no reason other than they were bored of having them around." He looked down at the dog walking alongside Emily. "Beagles can be difficult to train if you don't know what you're doing. They're very lively."

"Do we need to get her to the vet?" asked Emily.

"Not just yet. Mike Turner's coming by this morning anyway. He's checking up on a couple of the boarders. I think she'll survive until then."

They reached the Range Rover. "Emily, do you want to go in the car with the dog?" asked Neil. "I'll follow behind. It might be too crowded with both of our bikes in there."

Emily settled in the backseat of the Range Rover with the dog's white-and-brown head resting on her lap. "I think she knows we're going to help her," she said, tracing the white diamond on her forehead.

Bob thanked Mrs. Paget for her help before getting into the front seat of the car and starting the engine.

Neil tapped on the window. "See you back at the house. I'll be right behind you." He stepped back and stood on the side of the road with his bike as the car slowly pulled away. Neil was relieved that at least the dog felt secure with someone.

CHAPTER TWO

Neil swerved into the driveway of his home at King Street Kennels and leaned his bike against a parked car. Carole Parker had been waiting outside when Bob and Emily arrived back with the dog. She looked a little anxious, but grinned cheerfully when she saw Neil. A small Pekingese was wriggling under her arm. "Phew! It's so busy today!" she said. "Two more dogs were dropped off while you were out."

Emily gently lifted the beagle down from the back-seat of the Range Rover.

"What have you brought us today?" asked Carole. "I only sent you out for a card for Kate's birthday." Kate McGuire was the King Street kennel assistant and was almost like one of the family.

Neil explained what had happened as they walked

to the rescue center. Set a bit further back from the house and main kennel blocks, the rescue center was a low, square building adjacent to the Parker's impressive-looking new barn, where Bob Parker held his twice-weekly training classes.

It didn't take Neil and Emily long to settle the beagle into one of the empty pens. The rescue center was funded by the local council and had room for ten lost or abandoned dogs. Everyone worked tirelessly to help find new owners for them.

Emily knelt beside the beagle, stroking her smooth coat. "I'm sure no one would deliberately abandon you. Someone must be looking for you, somewhere."

The beagle was lying on a soft blanket in the basket that Emily had put out for her. Her head was resting on her stretched-out paws. She looked up at them but didn't move. A ripple of a sigh seemed to run along her entire body.

Neil placed a metal bowl of water and a small dish of food in front of the dog. "Dad says that we shouldn't overfeed her. We'll let her rest for awhile. Mike Turner will be here soon to look her over. Come on, Em, she needs some peace."

The beagle began eating hungrily from the dish as Neil and Emily left the rescue center. They were walking back toward the house when they met Bob coming out of the kennel office shaking his head. "I've been in touch with Sergeant Moorhead and the

SPCA," he said. "There haven't been any missing beagles reported in this area for some time."

"What do you think could have happened to her collar and name tag?" asked Emily, anxiously. "They don't usually just fall off by themselves."

Bob Parker shrugged. "I have no idea. It may have been torn off. Or somebody could have removed it. I've asked Mike to bring his scanner to see if she has an identification chip."

"Don't worry," said Neil, squeezing his sister's arm gently. "She's going to be fine."

Mike Turner arrived at King Street Kennels in the late afternoon. Neil and Emily rushed out of the house when they heard his car pull up, and were closely followed by five-year-old Sarah — the baby of the family. Sarah ran up to the vet and insisted on helping him with his bag.

Bob Parker emerged from the kennel office and greeted his friend. "Mike. Glad you could make it."

"Sorry I'm late. There was an emergency at Priorsfield Farm," the vet explained. "One of Harry Gray's sheep got caught up in some wire fencing." He thanked Sarah for her help and ruffled her hair affectionately. "Now, what have you got for me today?"

"How about a basset hound with a grass seed in her ear?" said Bob, smiling.

Mike laughed. "Interesting. Anything else?"

"I'm a bit worried about a Great Dane, too. It's the first time she's boarded with us. She's hardly eating anything and I'd like you to check her out."

"We need you at the rescue center first, though," said Emily quickly.

Neil and Emily led the way to the beagle's pen. Mike Turner crouched down and peered inside at the frightened dog.

"We found her on the hill a couple of miles up the road toward Compton," said Emily. "She caused a car accident, but I don't think she was injured. She's probably more frightened than anything else, but she's so quiet. I'm really worried about her, Mike."

"No one seems to have reported her missing locally, either. We're just hoping she may have been microchipped," added Neil.

"Let's take a look at her," said Mike, stepping inside the pen. Emily followed him inside. The beagle licked Emily's outstretched hand. But when the vet came closer, the dog began to back away.

Mike squatted down beside the dog. "Come on, girl, I'm not going to hurt you. You'd better hold her for me, Emily." The beagle was trembling.

"She seems to trust Emily," said Neil, watching through the wire mesh.

Mike Turner gave the beagle a thorough examination. He gently felt her for any signs of injury. He listened to her heart and lungs with his stethoscope. Then he used a scanner to check for any signs that a tiny identity chip had been implanted in the rough folds of skin at the back of her neck. At last, the vet stood up. "We'll leave her alone now. She needs to sleep."

Outside the rescue center, Mike shook his head. "No luck with the scanner, I'm afraid. Her identity is still a mystery. That distinctive diamond shape on her head should help when you describe her to people, though. She's very weak and dehydrated, but I can't see anything more serious."

"Is she going to be all right?" asked Emily, anxiously.

"I think so. Beagles are a tough, sturdy breed. They've been bred for hunting hares and have a lot of stamina. She'll need a special diet and vitamins over the next week or so to build up her strength

again, but she should recover very quickly. It's difficult to tell how long she's been neglected and on the
run." The vet paused for a second. "But one thing I
can say for sure is that she's got quite a young litter
of puppies out there somewhere."

"Puppies!" said Neil and Emily at the same time.

"Yes, and I hate to think what kind of state they
may be in. She only stopped feeding them very recently. Her milk hasn't properly dried up yet. I don't
think the pups are much more than six or seven
weeks old."

"Hardly old enough to be without their mother,"
said Emily, quietly. "We should go and look for them.
They might be wandering around in the fields near
where we found her."

"Possibly. They may well be in need of my attention." The vet began to scribble in a notebook. "The
mother here will certainly be a beautiful dog when
she's in good condition again."

"I bet she has a decent pedigree. She looks pure-
bred. Best beagle I've seen for ages. Her puppies are
probably quite valuable," said Bob.

"Emily and I will go out and look around for
them," said Neil. "We've got to find them."

Mike nodded. "I think you're right. Now, Bob,
where are those other dogs you've got for me?"

Bob and Mike walked off toward the kennel
blocks.

Kate McGuire called out to Neil and Emily as they

were heading across the courtyard toward the house. Long strands of blond hair had escaped from her ponytail and she was looking a bit frazzled. Four eager dogs were straining at their leashes, impatient for their walk. "Neil! Emily! I'm just taking these four out for some exercise."

"Great," said Neil. "Sam could do with a run. And we need to go out anyway."

"We're on a mission," said Emily, seriously.

"What do you mean?" asked Kate.

Neil leaned inside the kitchen and unhooked Sam's leash from behind the door. "Can we take a

different route, Kate? We need to find a litter of beagle pups who've lost their mom."

A few minutes later they were in an open field, heading toward the hill where Neil and Emily had found the beagle mother. The sun was burning down and they were grateful for the light breeze that helped keep them cool. Neil grinned as he watched Sam bounding backward and forward along the path that ran adjacent to the road. The sheepdog's sleek black-and-white coat shone in the sunlight and his wet, black nose quivered at every new smell. He, at least, was in peak condition.

"Here, boy!" Neil called. Sam darted forward to his side, wagging his tail ecstatically as Neil ruffled his ears. He could feel the dog trembling with anticipation. Sam's bright, intelligent eyes stared up at him, waiting intently for Neil's next instruction; waiting to be released to continue his run. "OK, boy! Off you go!"

Sam shot away like an arrow.

"This is it," said Emily, as they climbed over a fence that brought them into the cornfield they had been in that morning.

Neil scanned the field. "There's not much cover, is there? Where could the pups be hiding — if they're even still here?"

Kate glanced around. "Let's try looking along the bushes and in the field across the road, too."

After what seemed like ages searching under every thorny bush and tree, Emily wiped her brow, flopped down into some long grass, and sighed. "Nothing. Absolutely nothing."

Neil shrugged and kicked at a chunk of mud on the ground. "We tried our best, Emily. We had to be sure they weren't here."

"Then where are they?"

Kate sat down on a tree stump and patted one of the dogs panting near her feet — a hairy, gray miniature schnauzer. "Come on, you two. Don't get too upset about it. I'm sure you'll think of some other way of tracking them down." Kate smiled. "You always do. Let's go up to the ridge and give the dogs a good run before we head back."

Neil and Emily picked themselves up and dusted themselves off. "OK."

"I'm glad we're nearly at the top," Kate puffed, as she climbed the final few yards toward the top of the Compton Vale ridge. "Is it just me or does this hill get steeper every time?"

"It's the heat," said Neil. "I only hope it stays like this for the rest of the summer."

On top of the ridge, Neil turned around a few times and admired the view. In the distance, he could see Compton. He picked out his school and the tall spire of the parish church.

Emily pointed out the field where they had just

been looking for the pups. "It's a good thing we found their mother when we did. I don't know how much longer she'd have lasted in this heat without water."

Kate nodded and sat down on a huge rock to catch her breath. "It'll be tough on the puppies, too. I hope they're getting regular drinks of water. I wonder what could have happened to them?"

"Surely no one would *dump* a litter of puppies," pondered Neil, rubbing his aching feet. "Although I've never heard of anyone *losing* a whole litter of puppies, either. I suppose they could still be with the owners."

"Yes, but if the owners have the puppies," said Emily, "why aren't they searching for the mother? It just doesn't make sense. I'm sure the puppies are somehow the key to it all."

"Neither of you can remember anything about lost beagle pups in the *Compton News*?" asked Kate, placing the handle loops of her dog leashes over her foot. She didn't want any of the dogs running away.

Emily frowned and thought hard. "Not me." The Parkers checked the lost-and-found column in the *Compton News* every week.

"Me, neither," said Neil, scratching his chin. "Nothing specifically about missing puppies, anyway." Suddenly his face lit up. "Hang on. I'm sure I remember a news item, though. I think it was something about a *pregnant* dog that had been missing. A dog *about* to have puppies!" He stood up excitedly.

"We have to get back. I've got to look it up. It might be the same dog!" Neil ran headlong down the hill with Sam barking excitedly at his heels. Kate and Emily followed him and tried to keep up.

"Neil, what are you talking about?" asked Emily, breathlessly.

"Don't you remember? A woman had contacted a bunch of local papers because she was so desperate to find her missing dog."

"And the dog was definitely about to have puppies?" questioned Kate, running alongside Neil. Her four dogs were thoroughly enjoying this renewed burst of energy at the end of their long walk.

"Yes. That's what made it stick out in my mind. It might even have been a beagle. We could have solved this already!"

CHAPTER THREE

Neil rushed through the back door at King Street Kennels, and hastily filled up Sam's bowl with water, spilling it all over the kitchen floor. "Whoops! Sorry, Sam! Got to run." The collie lapped it up thirstily, ignoring Neil's strange behavior. Neil charged into the kitchen and immediately bumped into Sarah and his mom who were on their way out.

"Watch out!" said Carole. "What's your hurry?"

"Newspapers!" Neil bounced around the kitchen grabbing every paper he could lay his hands on. He took some from a pile under the sink and others from a box in the cupboard. Soon he had a huge, unsteady pile in his arms.

"Those are Fudge's!" shrieked Sarah. Neil's sister was very attached to her pet hamster and hated to think that her big brother was taking away his future bedding.

"Fudge can have them back as soon as I've looked through them — and he'd better not have had the one I need," snapped Neil.

"Neil's being nasty," wailed Sarah.

"Not really, sweetheart," said Carole. "I think he's just looking for something. There are some more papers upstairs, Neil."

"Thanks!"

When they left, Neil spread the papers on the kitchen table.

Emily sat beside him and grabbed a paper from the pile. "What exactly are we looking for?"

"A news feature about a missing dog from up north somewhere. Was it Middlesbrough?"

"But, Neil, that's over a hundred miles away. It can't be the dog we found."

"From what I remember, the owner couldn't find it locally. She'd tried everything," said Neil excitedly. "That's why she widened the search."

"Well, let's look through these papers first. How long ago was it?"

Neil shrugged. "I'm not sure. A month. Maybe two. I think it was before spring break."

"There are hardly any from that far back, anyway. We won't bother with anything before May. Put those in a pile on the floor. Then we'll start reading. Was there a picture of the dog?"

"I think so," said Neil, opening the first paper and beginning to scan the pages.

Neil and Emily were still reading when Carole Parker and Sarah returned home an hour later. Neil was looking very dejected. "It's no use," he said. "It's not here. There are lots of issues missing. Sarah must have used it for her stupid hamster. I really thought we were onto something."

"Come on, Neil," said his mom. "That's unfair. It's not Sarah's fault. She's *supposed* to use the old papers."

Sarah was looking quite upset.

"Sorry," Neil mumbled.

"What's this all about, anyway?" Carole Parker asked.

Neil told her about the article. His mom shook her head. "It seems a bit of a long shot to me. Middlesbrough is so far away. Why would the dog have strayed here? In any case, if it was that long ago, she probably would have turned up by this time."

"The dog might have been stolen. It could be anywhere by now. There's no reason why it couldn't be the one we found."

"Take a look at the clippings file in the office, too," said Carole. "I can't remember anything about a beagle, or beagle pups, but you never know."

Neil shook his head. "I'm convinced I remember a *news* story, not a mention in the lost-and-found column."

"We should look in the back issues of the paper in the library," suggested Emily.

Neil brightened. "Good idea, Em. Let's go." Neil got up and scraped his chair along the wooden kitchen floor.

"Neil, it's Saturday afternoon — the library will be closed."

Neil sat back down again. There was nothing more he could do.

"Is it always this hectic in July?" asked Carole Parker. "I can't remember a Saturday as busy as this for ages." Everyone was sitting in the kitchen taking a well-earned rest.

"Yes," Bob and Kate agreed.

"And there are still two new arrivals to come," said Carole, taking a sip from her steaming cup of coffee.

"It's not usually this hot, though," said Emily, wiping her forehead dramatically.

"I've felt really sticky all day," added Neil.

"Fudge is sweating, too," said Sarah, slurping her lemonade noisily.

"Hamsters don't sweat, silly," scolded Neil.

"I'd keep checking that his water bottle's full, if I were you," said Bob Parker.

"How's the beagle doing?" asked Carole.

"She was asleep when I last looked in," said Neil. "Mike says that she needs all the rest she can get after what she's been through."

"She certainly hasn't been getting the right kind of food. I don't think she's eaten at all for a few days," said Bob.

Emily sighed. "Someone must be really worried about her. I hope her puppies are managing to fend for themselves."

"I'm afraid we won't know until we find them," replied Bob. "But at least a lot of people are on the lookout for them, and it's not easy to hide a whole litter of hungry pups."

"I'm sure she's the dog from that article," Neil insisted. "If only we could make a wider appeal for information about her. You know, Dad, if only we had a modem and a scanner for the computer . . ." He glanced at his father sheepishly.

"Not that one again!" laughed Bob Parker.

"No, seriously, Dad. If we created our own King Street Kennels website, we would be able to scan in pictures of any lost dogs that we found. People looking for a dog anywhere in England would be able to visit our website to see if we had found it."

"From anywhere in the *world*," added Emily.

"It would help promote our business, too," Neil persisted. "Really, Dad. More and more people are getting access to the Internet. There's even a Select-a-Dog site — a database to help match people to the right kind of pet. You answer questions such as, how experienced you are, how big your backyard is, and how much exercise you would be able to give a dog."

Bob Parker nodded. "Well, I'm all for that. The rescue center might not be so busy if people didn't take on the wrong kind of dog in the first place."

"So does that mean we can have one then?" asked Neil.

"No."

Carole smiled. "It sounds like a great idea, Neil. I'm sure there are lots of practical uses we could put it to. But there just isn't any money around for it at the moment."

Neil made a face.

Emily looked out of the window dreamily. "It would be so cool. There are lots of wildlife sites to visit. And chat rooms where you can talk to other people who love dogs. We could get campaigns and petitions organized, and send e-mail . . ."

Sam poked his snout out from underneath the table and barked, as if in agreement.

"You see, even Sam thinks it's a good idea!" Neil laughed.

"Wait a minute! I don't know about you, Carole, but I feel like we're being ganged up on here!" Bob chuckled.

Carole Parker sat back in her chair. "The fact is, we can't afford it. Rebuilding the barn after the fire this year was really expensive, even though the insurance money paid for most of it."

"It's just that we want to help the rescue center dogs as much as possible," said Emily.

"And we *really* want to find the beagle puppies," added Neil.

"I know," Carole said, sympathetically. "Look, why don't you go over to the exercise field and fill up Sarah's old kiddie pool for Sam. He'd enjoy a splash in that and it might help you cool down, too."

"Good idea," said Neil.

Sarah jumped up. "And me! Please, Neil, please let me!"

Neil looked at Emily and groaned. It was going to be a long night.

On Sunday morning, a loud chorus of barking signaled the early arrival of Kate McGuire. Neil was lying awake in his bed. He felt like rolling over and trying to go back to sleep, but his thoughts kept turning to the lost dog in the rescue center. Where had she come from? If only he could find the beagle's owner and locate her missing puppies. Monday — his next opportunity to look through some more newspapers — seemed so far away.

An urgent knocking on the front door of the house interrupted his thoughts. Neil heard his dad stumbling down the stairs, then Kate's voice. She sounded worried.

"Sorry, Bob, I thought I should wake you. There's something here you should see."

Neil leaped out of bed, scrambled into some

clothes, and ran downstairs. Something was going on that he didn't want to miss.

"What is it, Kate?" came Bob's bleary voice. "What's the problem?"

"Come and see." Kate beckoned Bob outside and Neil slipped into the fresh morning air before the door was closed behind them.

Kate was standing by the main gatepost at the entrance to the driveway. Tied to it was a whimpering cocker spaniel puppy. Its owner was nowhere in sight.

CHAPTER FOUR

Kate untied the dog and gently lifted it up into her arms. Almost at once, the dog stopped making any noise. "I spotted him as soon as I arrived. I don't think he's been there long." The puppy's dark, sorrowful eyes were looking up at her. His black-and-white flecked coat was badly matted. Kate stroked his long silky ears. "There's a good boy. Don't be scared," she cooed.

"He's a blue roan, isn't he?" Neil whispered. "He's fantastic." The dog's mixture of black and white hairs looked gray in the early light. A white star of fur twinkled on the top of his smooth black head.

Bob Parker coughed. "We'd better get him inside. He must be only about six months old." Mr. Parker held out his hand for the puppy to sniff. "I bet you can be a bit of a rascal, can't you? Was he left with a note or anything, Kate?"

Kate shook her head. "There wasn't anything tied to the gate."

"Look, Dad," said Neil. "There's something attached to his collar."

"Put him down, Kate, and we'll have a look."

Kate held the puppy's leash while Neil tried to unravel a small twisted plastic bag from his collar. Once he was on the floor, the puppy wouldn't keep still. He seemed more intent on scrambling over Neil's shoes and jumping up to lick his face than allowing him to inspect his collar. "Hey! Keep still. Ouch!" Neil yelled as the young dog playfully nipped his fingers. At last, he managed to detach the bag and he tore it open. A handful of coins clattered onto the floor.

"They must have left this money for his food," said Kate.

Bob Parker shrugged. "It won't go very far."

"At least they've tried to do something right, Dad," said Neil. "This must be better than just putting him on the side of the road."

"True. You're right, Neil. I just wish people would consider the consequences before taking on a puppy. The trouble with cocker spaniels is that they look absolutely adorable, and they are extremely affectionate — but they're often high-strung and excitable, too. They have a lot of energy and can be a real handful."

"As we've just found out," said Neil.

After breakfast, Neil and Emily watched the cocker spaniel through the wire mesh of his new home in the rescue center. The puppy rattled around in his pen, eagerly pouncing on a rubber ball and a squeaky bone. Then he stopped running and sat looking around, as if he was slightly puzzled.

"What's he got in his mouth?" asked Emily, tilting her head to one side to try and make out what the object was.

Neil chuckled. "It's one of Dad's slippers. He grabbed it when we were walking him over here earlier this morning. Time to get it back, I think."

"How are we going to do that? He looks pretty attached to it."

Neil grinned. "Watch." He opened the door of the pen and stepped inside. Kneeling down, he fished out a small doggie treat from his pocket and held it between his fingers in his outstretched hand. "Here, boy."

The pup immediately dropped the slipper and dived for the treat. "Thank you!" said Neil triumphantly. He grabbed the slipper and Emily started clapping. Having wolfed down the treat, the puppy looked around for the missing slipper.

"I'm impressed," said Emily. "But what would you have done if the puppy hadn't been hungry?"

"I've never known a cocker spaniel that wasn't! I suspect he's been grabbing and chewing everything he could get his paws on since he was born. Come on, let's go and see Kate. She'll be getting the meals ready and we can help with the beagle."

They found Kate measuring out dog food for the boarders. She knew the requirements for the regulars, but a couple of new dogs were on diets she hadn't prepared before. The dogs were always fed whatever they were used to at home.

"Hi! Do you think you could take care of feeding Ben for me?" Kate looked up from her clipboard. "Here's his bowl. Julie told you what he eats, didn't she? He needs some water, too."

"Sure," said Emily, grabbing scoops of dog food

from one of the bags. "No problem." Ben was a big, shaggy Old English sheepdog that belonged to one of Emily's best friends from school. Julie had gone on vacation to Scotland and Emily had promised to take extra-special care of him.

"I'll feed the beagle," volunteered Neil.

"Great," said Kate. "You can make up her food yourself. Mike Turner's left her some special supplements. I've got the instructions here. She's got to have four small meals a day to build up her strength."

Neil clutched some dishes of food and water, then walked quickly over to the rescue center. Most of the dogs knew it was feeding time and were making a lot of noise as he approached. "Be quiet!" he yelled jokingly, as he kicked open the main door with his foot.

The beagle was curled up in her basket. Her tan head, topped with its long rounded ears and a white diamond, was resting on her paws. Her eyes were open and she looked up at Neil as he quietly opened the pen.

Emily joined him after feeding Ben and knelt down by the dog's basket. She gently began to stroke her ears. "We brought you some food," she whispered. The beagle's eyes had a sad, pleading expression and Emily would have given anything to see just one wag of her white-tipped tail, but she didn't move.

"I put the food down here, Em. Let's leave her and see what she does."

They waited quietly outside the pen. Slowly the beagle uncurled and stretched herself. She climbed out of the basket and walked unsteadily toward the food. Then she began to eat, hesitantly at first, but then with increasing assurance. A couple of minutes later, the bowl was empty. She moved to her water and began to drink. She paused and looked up at them.

"Good girl!" whispered Emily, encouragingly.

Neil thought he saw the faintest hint of a tail wag as the beagle put her head down again and continued drinking.

When she had finished, the beagle began to pace inside the pen, sniffing the ground where Neil and Emily had walked. Then she seemed to lose interest. She climbed into her basket and curled up tightly.

"Do you think she misses her puppies?" asked Emily as they walked back to the house.

"I don't know. Puppies aren't usually fully weaned until seven or eight weeks, and even then they still spend some time with their mother." Neil sighed. "I just wish we could find out what's happened to them."

The highlight of Sunday afternoon for Sarah was helping to wash and trim the young spaniel puppy abandoned at the Parkers' front gate. The highlight for Neil was *watching* Sarah help wash and trim the spaniel — he knew it was going to be very messy and very funny.

Neil sat the puppy on the treatment table in the kennel storeroom. All the grooming equipment was kept here. There was a bath basin and a grooming table and a special drying cabinet, which they used in the winter.

Sarah wanted to help Kate on her own, but another pair of more experienced hands was definitely necessary. "I'll have to hold him for Kate," Neil told her. "But you can help rub in the shampoo. We don't know yet whether he likes to have baths."

The puppy loved the water. "He looks like a little otter!" Sarah giggled, peering into the dog bath to rub noses with him. The puppy leaped up at her, scrabbling at the sides of the bath basin.

"He looks more like a drowned rabbit with long droopy ears," said Neil.

Once or twice, the squirming puppy slipped from Sarah's gentle grasp and splashed everybody with waves of soapy water. Neil finally caught and covered the puppy with a large towel. Sarah helped rub him dry after his bath and Kate helped to dry Sarah. Neil wiped down the table and other surfaces that got wet in the process.

Kate ran her fingers through the tangled black-and-gray puppy fur — the long hair on his legs and chest and tummy was completely matted.

"How are we going to get those tangles out?" asked Neil.

Kate shook her head. "We can't. The conditioner I used hasn't made any difference. He should have been groomed every day to keep his coat free of knots." She tugged on the bits of long hair on the puppy's legs and tummy. "I'll have to shave them off with the electric clipper."

"You can't shave him!" protested Sarah. "I don't want him to be bald!"

"He won't be bald," said Kate, reaching for the electric clipper that was hanging on a hook on the wall. "And his hair will grow long again soon. If you help me brush him every day, we'll manage to keep him free of tangles. The noise may scare him a bit so we'll have to work very slowly to start with. Here, Sarah," she said, handing her some dog treats. "I want you to be ready with these."

Neil held the little spaniel while Kate switched on the clipper. The black-and-white puppy jumped nervously at the noise. Kate nodded to Sarah. "OK, give him one of the treats."

While the puppy munched the treat, Kate gently began to shave one leg. Then she told Sarah to give him another. "That's a good boy!" said Kate moving onto the puppy's next leg. "This way the puppy learns that it really isn't too bad, being clipped."

When Kate had finished, the table was covered with piles of matted fur. Neil lifted the pup gently down to the floor. Then the spaniel scampered away, shaking himself, pleased to be free.

"He'll feel better in this heat without that thick coat," said Neil, admiring their handiwork. They watched as the newly shorn puppy ran around the room. His legs looked very thin and spindly and his body looked like a smooth, round barrel.

Sarah laughed. "Look at him! He looks just like a little, black lamb! Can we call him Baa?"

Neil and Kate exchanged glances but both ended up smiling. "OK. Baa it is," agreed Neil. It was common practice to give names to all the unclaimed dogs in the rescue center and Neil suddenly found himself thinking about the beagle again. They hadn't given her a name yet. Somehow it hadn't felt right. She still had a name of her own. He was sure that somewhere, someone was thinking about her, still using that name, hoping that they would one day find her.

Through the window, they saw a gray Honda drive up. Neil thought it looked familiar. Kate glanced at her watch. "Is that the time already? I've got to run, Neil. A friend is coming to pick me up. Can you and Sarah take Baa back to the rescue center?"

"Sure."

Neil stepped outside and watched Kate run up and greet the young man who got out of the car. He was tall and well-built, with a baggy white T-shirt. His blond hair was long and swept back. Neil guessed that he was a couple of years older than

Kate. She waved at Neil to come over. Glancing over his shoulder to check that Sarah and Baa were happily inside the storeroom playing together, he went over to join them.

"Neil, this is Glenn," said Kate, introducing the man. He cracked a wide smile and shook Neil's hand.

"Good to meet you, Neil. Kate says you know as much as she does about dogs. Almost!"

Neil laughed. "I taught her everything she knows, Glenn!"

"I'll leave my bike here today, Neil. Glenn can give me a lift back tomorrow."

Bob Parker emerged from the office. "Hope the meeting goes well. Fill me in on what happens next time I see you."

Glenn nodded his head. "Great, I'll be glad to." He jumped into the car and closed the door. Kate waved from the passenger seat as they drove off.

"What meeting? Where are they going, Dad?" Neil asked.

"Glenn's a student at Padsham Agricultural College. Apparently there's some concern that Universal Laboratories, the new research center on the main road outside Padsham, may be testing cosmetics on animals. Glenn belongs to an animal protection group that has some inside information on it."

"Who was that?" asked Emily, appearing beside them. "He looked pretty cute!"

"Kate's new boyfriend," said Neil, matter-of-factly. "He says the new research center is using animals to test makeup."

"Just a second, Neil," said Bob Parker. "He said they *might* be using animals. We don't know anything for certain yet. And we don't know that he's actually Kate's boyfriend!"

Neil nudged his sister in the ribs. "Dad, get real! Of course, he is. You should have seen her jump when his car arrived."

"Well, regardless, do you remember Mrs. Paget?" said Bob. "She was the woman who stopped to help you with the beagle yesterday. She's Glenn's mom."

"I thought the car looked familiar. She had that damage fixed up pretty quickly."

Emily was hardly listening. She was remembering a television documentary she had seen recently where a laboratory had been infiltrated and exposed for its abuse of animals. She could see the pictures now — rows and rows of cages. Dogs in cages. *Beagles* in cages. Beagles staring forlornly through iron bars; beagles with terrible sores on their backs, tubes being forced down their throats . . . It was all so horrible and cruel. And now a research center had opened just a few miles away, where they might be using animals, too.

Bob Parker looked at his watch and mumbled something about having to get back to work. He turned around and headed back toward the kennel office.

Emily remained rooted to the spot she stood in. She turned to her brother with an ashen face. "Neil," she said, quietly. "I think our lost beagle might have come from that place. She might have escaped from that new research center."

Neil stared at her and immediately understood what she was saying. "Do you think Universal Laboratories took the beagle to test makeup on her puppies?"

"It can't just be a coincidence. The puppies may still be there. We've got to get over there."

Neil frowned. "It's possible, I suppose. But what can we do?"

"I've got to see the place for myself. Can you imagine what they may be doing to those puppies right now?" Emily turned and ran to get her bike.

Neil stared after her anxiously. If there was a chance that the puppies were still alive, he had to help her. "Wait!" he called out. "I'm coming with you."

CHAPTER FIVE

The Universal Laboratories research center was on the outskirts of Padsham. Neil and Emily rode their bikes along the busy main road from Compton, full of slow-moving cars, and arrived outside exhausted. Set well back from the road, the large site on which the research center stood had been tastefully landscaped. Large mounds of earth were piled up to obscure the twisting complex of low buildings. A white sign, surrounded by a selection of brightly colored plants, stood at the beginning of the short driveway.

"Universal Laboratories," Emily read out loud. *"No unauthorized entry. All visitors must report to the reception area."*

"This is it, then," said Neil.

They leaned their bikes against some of the young

trees that had been planted in front of a tall fence. In a few years, the buildings wouldn't be noticeable at all from the road.

"It looks like a prison," whispered Emily breathlessly, looking up at the impenetrable barrier in front of them. The vast expanse of metal fencing was crowned by twists of menacing barbed wire.

Neil grabbed his bike again. "Come on, let's take a closer look."

Slowly, they began to push their bikes up the driveway toward the main gate. The white sentry-like box and road barrier were unmanned but the huge gates beyond were firmly closed.

"I guess they're not so busy on a Sunday. There's no one here. We can't possibly get in," said Emily.

Neil pointed to the surveillance cameras mounted high on the fence. "They sure didn't skimp on the security. They must have something to hide."

Suddenly, a slow whirring noise caught their attention. The nearest camera sprang to life and pivoted slowly toward them. Neil and Emily stood still for a moment and there was a strange silence. Their hearts thumped in time to a red light flashing on the side of the camera.

"I don't like this," whispered Emily, trying not to move her lips.

Neil was less cautious. "Ssh!" he signaled. His face had gone white. "Listen!"

Straining their ears, Neil and Emily detected a

sound. Barely audible, it was coming from some-where on the other side of the fence inside the complex. The low whining grew louder and more persistent.

Neil gripped the fence and strained to see. "Emily, they have dogs in there! I told you!"

As the whining gave way to a sudden angry bark, Emily vigorously pulled at Neil's sleeve. "Let's get out of here. There's nothing we can do."

Neil looked around but still couldn't see where the noise was coming from. He reluctantly loosened his grip and allowed Emily to pull him away.

They scrambled onto their bikes and rejoined the passing weekend traffic.

Half an hour later, downing cold drinks and trying to cool off, Neil and Emily were sitting in the kitchen at King Street Kennels. "Why would Universal Labora-tories have all that security?" asked Neil, gulping back his third glass of water. "I'm sure something's going on in there. How are we going to get the pup-pies out?"

"We're still not sure they're in there, Neil. We heard barking, not little puppy yaps. Maybe Kate and Glenn will be able to tell us more tomorrow, af-ter their meeting," said Emily.

Their conversation was interrupted by Sarah's ar-rival. She burst through the kitchen door crying and dramatically flung herself across the kitchen table between them. Carole Parker followed her inside.

"They're going to take Baa away," Sarah wailed.

"Oh, come on, Sarah," said Carole. "Those people haven't come especially for *him*. They might choose *any* dog. You know your father won't let a dog go to a home unless he feels it's right."

"But Baa's so sweet, they'll want him and *I* love him," she cried.

Carole Parker glanced at Neil and Emily. They seemed uninterested in Sarah's emotional antics. "What's the matter with you two?" she asked.

"We've been over to the new research center in Padsham," said Emily. "We think they might have the beagle puppies."

"Really?" replied Carole, sounding slightly aston-
ished. "You've been all the way over there?"

"It's like a prison. It's awful," Neil blurted out. "We
definitely heard dogs barking. You've heard what
they do. They put chemicals into rabbits' eyes to see
if they go blind, they shut dogs up in small cages and
force them to eat poison, they do terrible things to
mice and rats . . ."

"Neil!" said his mother sharply, nodding toward
Sarah as a fresh round of wailing broke out from the
table. She was wide-eyed and had been listening to
every word.

"I won't let them hurt Fudge!" cried Sarah.

"Don't worry, Squirt," Emily said, rubbing her sister's shoulder. "No one's going to touch Fudge."

"I've read that a lot of animals do get stolen for research," said Neil. "If they stole the beagle for her
puppies, then we've got to rescue them."

"Bob!" cried Carole as her husband walked
through the door. "Can you help me out here?"

Sarah picked herself up and ran to Bob, clutching
at his legs and sobbing, "I don't want Baa to go to a
new home yet!"

Bob Parker lifted her up. "Baa's not ready to go
away yet, and he's not really suitable for that family.
They've never had a dog before and the woman quite
liked the thought of taking the collie who came in
last week. She's a lot older and has already been

trained." He turned to Neil. "They're coming back next week. Maybe you could take her out into the exercise field with them when they do, Neil. Neil?"

Neil was staring at the kitchen table.

Carole sighed and looked across at Bob. "It's this research center. They're getting very worked up over it."

Bob sat down at the table. "Come on, guys, we don't really have any facts yet. We don't know for sure that animals are being used for testing cosmetics. If it does turn out that they are, then we'll do all we can to help Glenn with his campaign. There's no justification for any animal being made to suffer so that people can make themselves look better."

"But we have to help the beagle puppies *now,*" insisted Neil. "We have no idea what's already been done to them."

"I can't believe they really have those puppies, Neil," said Bob. "I'm not even sure that dogs are used for cosmetics testing anymore. Give it a rest, OK? We're doing all we can to help the beagle. We've alerted all the agencies about her and the puppies, and you're going to check out that article in the library tomorrow. I'm sure something's going to come up soon."

Neil got up and pushed his chair away. "Well, there must be *something* I can do."

"Where are you going?" asked Emily anxiously.

"To check those newspapers again. Anything's better than sitting around here doing nothing." Neil picked up his drink and marched out of the room.

Emily smiled at her dad sheepishly and then followed Neil.

CHAPTER SIX

The next day, Neil and Emily were up early. They wanted to spend some more time with the beagle before the library opened and make sure her recovery was going according to plan.

The beagle greeted them with a slow wag of her tail when they opened her door in the rescue center. She sat down at Emily's feet and lifted one paw.

"Neil! Look! I think she's getting used to us," said Emily, crouching down and gently shaking the paw.

"She's showing us what she can do. You're a clever girl, aren't you?"

The beagle nestled up against Emily. She rested her head on Emily's knee and then tried to sniff and lick Neil's hand when he stroked her long, silky ears. This time, she didn't back away. "I think she knows we're trying to help her," said Neil. "She likes us. She's getting her strength back — just as Mike predicted."

"She's beautiful, too," said Emily, smiling. "When she's fully recovered and back with her pups she'll be even better."

Neil looked at his watch. "C'mon. Breakfast first, then we'll head off into town. We've got to find that article." He stroked the beagle again. "For her sake."

Neil and Emily sat waiting on the steps of the Compton Library fifteen minutes before opening time. The beagle had been in and out of Neil's thoughts since Saturday. "We've been through the other papers at home twice now and there's definitely nothing in them about the beagle," said Neil wearily.

"You start on the ones we haven't read and I'll see what books they've got on cosmetic testing," said Emily. "I want to find the rules and regulations about what you can test on different animals."

After what seemed like an eternity, the heavy wooden doors of the library creaked open and the librarian beckoned them in. Once inside, they separated and Neil headed toward the local reference section where back issues of the *Compton News* were kept. When he found the file he wanted, he took it and sat at a large oak table near the shelves. He began to read the first newspaper, scanning and turning each page as quickly as he could.

Ten minutes later, a whoop of delight from Neil brought Emily running in from the next room. "I've got it, Em!" he cried.

The librarian behind the front desk peered at them disapprovingly.

"Sorry," whispered Neil. He turned to Emily, pointed at the open newspaper spread out in front of him, and tried to talk more quietly. "The article's so small I nearly missed it. There's no picture, either. It's dated the beginning of June. I think that's about right."

Emily peered over his shoulder. "What does it say?"

"Listen to this. The article's headline is *Missing from Middlesbrough . . . In a desperate hunt for her missing dog, Mrs. Joan Thompson has contacted more than one hundred newspapers across the north and northwest regions. Bella, her daughter's four-year-old champion beagle, has been missing for two weeks. All attempts to find Bella in her local area have failed. Concern is growing because Bella is due to have puppies within the next couple of days. 'We're devastated,' said Mrs. Thompson, 42, of Ayresome Park Road. 'Bella belongs to my nine-year-old daughter, Sally. The dog was my husband's last present to her before he died.'*"

"That's awful," said Emily. "Sally's my age. She must be so upset. Wouldn't it be wonderful if we really had found her dog?" Emily paused. "But if it is

Bella, how could she have gotten all the way down here?"

Neil looked at Emily. "She was stolen by the research center, of course." He began scanning the page again. "There's no phone number here. How are we going to get in touch with the owner? And I'm sure I remember a picture of a dog."

"Jake might be able to help us out," suggested Emily. Neil and Emily often asked the friendly local photographer at the *Compton News* to feature adoptable dogs from the rescue center in the newspaper. "He might know someone who could tell us more."

Neil shook his head. "No, he's on vacation. Three weeks in France. I remember him saying he wouldn't be back until next week."

"Oh. Maybe there's another article later on, then. C'mon, we'll both look," said Emily, grabbing some of the papers.

Half an hour later, Neil and Emily had completed their search and not found any further mentions of Bella, the missing beagle. They were both feeling very dejected.

"We can't go through them again," said Neil. "We've read them from cover to cover already."

"And I didn't find any books on cosmetics testing, either," said Emily. "What are we going to do now?"

"No luck?" asked the librarian, who was stacking some nearby shelves. "If you're searching for something local, are you sure it was the *Compton News?* Have you tried the *Advertiser?*"

"The *Advertiser!*" yelled Neil, jumping up.

"Shh!" said Emily and the librarian together.

Neil didn't move. "What's the *Advertiser?*" he whispered.

"You know," said Emily. "That thin, free paper that gets shoved under our door every other week — if they remember to deliver it. It's mostly advertisements but there are some news stories in there."

"I'll get them for you." The librarian disappeared and came back a few minutes later with another pile of newspapers. "Try these," she said.

This time Emily nearly jumped out of her seat. She found what she was looking for in the first paper she picked up. "Look! Bella! There's a picture! It *is* her. The markings are the same. She has a diamond on her forehead! And see how that white bit on her chest comes around the left side of her neck."

"Let me see!" Neil could hardly contain himself. *"Reward offered for Missing Mom,"* Neil began. *"Owners lose hope for Bella the missing beagle . . . After six weeks on the run, hopes are fading for Bella and her newborn pups. Her owner has made a dramatic TV appeal for her return."*

"Is there a phone number?" asked Emily.

Neil scanned the rest of the article and nodded. "Yes, there is. Let's get this photocopied and get home. Do you have any change for the machine?"

While Neil was photocopying the article, the librarian came over to Emily with some leaflets. "I'm sorry we didn't have any books on what you wanted. Would these be of any help to you instead?" she asked. "We had quite a few copies left here the other day. There's a lot about animal testing in them."

"Thank you," said Emily, staring at the front of the leaflet. It was a flyer trying to bring attention to the issue of cosmetics research on animals. A national animal rights group based in Manchester had produced it. Emily's face dropped in dismay when she saw the pictures inside. Staring out at her was a beagle's face pressed up against the bars of a cage.

Bob and Carole Parker were in the office together checking through some paperwork when Neil and Emily got home. "We found it," shouted Neil, as he crashed in through the door. "I've got a number to call."

"There's a picture, too," said Emily. "We're sure it's the same dog. Her name is Bella."

"Let's see the picture," said Bob. He looked at it closely.

"See that bit there, Dad," said Emily. "The way the white sweeps around."

Bob nodded. "Yes, it's certainly similar. Well done. Give it a try!"

Neil tried the number. "It's ringing." He waited, holding the phone close to his ear. "No one's answering it."

"Keep trying," urged Emily. "They may be outside."

Neil hung on, growing increasingly impatient with every unanswered ring. He put the phone down and tried the number again. Still no reply. "It's no use," he said. "The owner's definitely not in."

"Never mind," said Carole. "Try again later. Don't be too disappointed. You've already made a fantastic breakthrough."

Neil shrugged, trying not to show how upset he was. "It would explain the dog taking a liking to Emily, wouldn't it? You know, if she'd belonged to a girl her age."

"It's possible," said Bob. "You'll also be interested to know that Glenn's coming over at lunchtime. He's got some news about what the research center is up to. It seems that they definitely *are* using some animals to test cosmetics."

"I knew it," said Neil, perking up. "We've got to get the puppies out of there." He ran toward the door. "I'm going to see what Kate knows."

"Wait!" called out Carole. "Kate is . . . Oh, never mind."

Neil had already disappeared.

Kate was out walking some of the boarding dogs. After a frustrating half hour kicking his heels, Neil rushed out of the house when he saw Glenn arriving on a bike. Kate came back just as Neil was eagerly ushering him into the kitchen.

"Thanks for dropping by, Glenn," Bob told him. "I think Neil and Emily have got some questions for you about last night's meeting."

"You've found something out, haven't you?" asked Neil.

"Well," said Glenn, nodding, "as Kate may have already told you, we now know for sure that Universal Laboratories has recently signed a contract with a large international cosmetics company called Custom Care Products. They're going to use animals to test a new waterproof mascara that the company currently has in development."

Bob interrupted. "I'm sorry, Glenn, but does this involve dogs? Neil seems to have the idea that the beagle we found the other day has come from there. He thinks the research center could be using her puppies."

"I really don't think so, Neil," said Glenn. "Although hundreds of animals are still used every year for cosmetics tests in this country, they're mostly guinea pigs and mice and rabbits. Dogs are only used for medical research now."

"Well, couldn't they be using them for that?" Neil persisted.

"And dogs and pets do get stolen for research," added Emily. "It says so in all the leaflets."

Neil reached under the table and stroked Sam's head. There is no way he would let anybody steal his dog.

Glenn continued his explanation. "Dogs are stolen sometimes, but not in this country. All animals used in laboratories have to come from special breeding establishments. I'm pretty sure your beagle and her puppies wouldn't have been stolen by the research center. It would be too much of a risk for them to take. There are some very strict laws governing exactly what these research labs can and can't use."

"No one's going to steal my Fudge, are they?" said Sarah.

Glenn smiled. "Definitely not, but we are trying to stop lots of rabbits and mice and hamsters like Fudge from being unnecessarily hurt and killed."

"What can we do?" asked Carole.

"We want to make sure that everyone knows what's going on. If there's enough negative publicity, the company and the center may be persuaded to abandon these kinds of tests. It's early enough for us to put a lot of pressure on them to give up this kind of work. There are lots of other methods of research these people can use." Glenn rummaged around in his bag and pulled out a bunch of bulging folders.

Kate leaned over Glenn's shoulder and opened up some of the folders. She spread out some leaflets across the table. "There are a lot of things we can all do to help. There's going to be a protest rally outside the center on Saturday. We need help getting signatures for a petition."

"Most of all, we need people to start boycotting all Custom Care products," said Glenn.

Neil and Emily picked up some of the leaflets. "Oh, no!" said Emily. "We've got some of this stuff in our bathroom!"

"There are a lot of companies who don't test their makeup on animals at all," said Kate. "We should all be using those. I've got a list here."

"I'll make a copy of that," said Carole. "I'm sure your aunt uses some of these products, Emily."

Emily turned to Glenn. Neil could see that his sister's brain was already working overtime. "We could make some huge signs for the rally. And I bet we can get lots of signatures, too."

"I can help," said Sarah. "I'll draw a giant picture of Fudge."

"Great," said Glenn. "Kate will keep you posted on any new plans or developments. Do you think you and Carole will be able to get to the rally, Bob?"

"We'll certainly try. One of us will have to stay at the kennel, but we'll do all we can."

"This is so exciting," cried Emily. "We can really make a difference!"

"We can — but not right now," said Bob, getting up from the table. "I think we'd better get back to work . . ."

Sarah turned to Kate. "I want Glenn to see Baa. Will he come?"

Glenn grinned. "Sure, I'll come. Kate's told me all about him."

"I'm going to start my sign now," said Emily. "I need to come up with a great slogan. Have you got any ideas, Neil?"

But Neil wasn't really listening. He was still thinking about Bella and her puppies. He wasn't completely reassured by what Glenn had said. "You know, Glenn, there *are* dogs there," he blurted out. "We heard them barking, didn't we, Em? Is there any way we can find out for sure that they're not using beagles?"

"You don't give up, do you?" said Glenn, smiling. "The barking you heard might have been guard dogs. They've got a couple of very fierce Dobermans patrolling day and night. If you're still really worried, I'll see what I can find out. That man who crashed into my mom the other day was actually the center's publicity officer. They're usually very careful about the information they release, but I might be able to find out something. I'll give you a call about it."

Neil watched from the doorstep as Sarah dragged Glenn and Kate away to visit Baa. Kate called to him. "Are you coming, Neil? We're giving him a run in the exercise field."

Neil shook his head. He wasn't in the mood. "No, I'm going to help Emily." He felt Sam brush against his legs. His alert, eager eyes were looking up expectantly at him. "Did you hear the word *run,* boy? Off you go then. Go and join them." He watched Sam race after Sarah and Kate.

Emily was already waving big bits of paper around in the kitchen. "Come on, Neil. I've got some great ideas for posters."

"In a minute," Neil replied. "I'm just going to call Mrs. Thompson again."

CHAPTER SEVEN

"**H**ave you tried getting hold of Bella's owners yet this morning, Neil?" asked Carole at breakfast.

Neil nodded. "Yes. I tried three times last night, and again this morning. There's still no answer. I'll try again in a minute."

"Finish your breakfast first or you'll be hungry later," Carole told him. Neil reluctantly went back to eating his cereal.

"Hello? Can everyone please hurry up?" Emily was hovering in the doorway with a large roll of cardboard tucked under her arm and a handful of thick markers. "I need this table to finish my poster."

Bob Parker popped his head through the kitchen doorway. "There's a visitor here for you, Neil."

Neil jumped up as his father showed a small,

blond-haired woman into the kitchen. "This is Mrs. Paget, Glenn's mom," Bob said, introducing her.

Mrs. Paget stretched out her hand. "Call me Wendy, please."

"And I'm Carole. Please, sit down. You've already met Neil and Emily," she said. "That's Sarah down there, I think," said Carole, pointing under the table. Sarah's foot and Sam's furry black tail could just be seen poking out into view.

Mrs. Paget smiled. "Sorry to barge in so early. Glenn was going to call Neil — but as I was passing . . ."

"Did he find out anything?" Neil interrupted eagerly. "He was going to call the man from the research center."

Mrs. Paget sat down at the table. "Yes, the man with the important meeting to go to. I called him last night. I needed to check something with him about the accident anyway. He had a police incident number I needed for my insurance claim."

"Was he still Mr. Angry?" asked Neil.

Wendy smiled. "Well, he wasn't very forthcoming to start with, but it helped that we'd met and he knew who I was. He wasn't prepared to go into details with me about any medical research they might or might not be doing involving animals. But when I mentioned beagle puppies, he did tell me something very interesting. It seems that a few days ago a man called up, actually trying to sell some beagle puppies to the research center!"

"I knew it! They've got them!" said Neil, energetically.

"Wait, hold on," said Mrs. Paget. "The center refused the man point-blank, of course. In fact, Mr. Pritchard wondered if the man was genuine at all, since all the animals they do use for experiments have to be legally obtained from specially licensed breeders. He suspected the man might be some activist trying to discredit the center. I assured him that the man didn't have anything to do with the protests."

"No," said Emily, grimly. "The man's genuine — whoever he is. And he still has Bella's puppies! We've got to find him."

Bob Parker nodded. "This looks like the lead you've both been waiting for. They could be the beagle's pups. It's too much of a coincidence and no reputable breeder would try and sell a litter in that fashion."

"I was reading through that leaflet Emily brought from the library," said Carole. "It can cost a lot to buy a beagle from a licensed breeder. He must have been hoping to make a lot of money from those puppies."

"What do you think he'll do now?" asked Emily. "They won't be worth much without pedigree documents."

"I doubt he'll just dump them," said Bob. "Even

without documents they're worth something to him. He might try to sell them as pets — especially if he's gone to the trouble and risk of stealing them. It's looking increasingly likely that Bella was stolen. She could have escaped from wherever the puppies are still being kept."

"But how are we going to find them?" Neil asked desperately.

"He might advertise them," suggested Mrs. Paget. "There are lots of ads in the papers. And the post office in Padsham is full of "for sale" notices advertising pets."

"Good idea," said Bob.

"We could try pet shops, too," exclaimed Emily.

"It looks like you and Neil have got your work cut out for you, Emily," said Carole. Then she turned to Mrs. Paget. "Thanks so much for all your help."

"Yes, you've been great," said Neil. He glanced at the kitchen clock on the wall. "I'll try that number again in Middlesbrough before we start looking. It's been at least half an hour since I last called."

A few minutes later, an elated Neil charged back into the room. "I got through! I got through! Someone answered."

"You spoke to Bella's owner? What did she say?" Emily asked excitedly.

"It wasn't Mrs. Thompson. It was a neighbor. She was feeding the cats when she heard the phone. Mrs.

Thompson and her daughter are away on vacation. And no, they haven't found Bella, she's still missing. They're coming back on Sunday. I left a message for her with our number."

"That's great, Neil," said Carole.

Wendy Paget got up. "Thanks for the coffee. I'm glad things are working out. Could I just take a quick look at Bella before I go? I'd like to see her again."

"Of course," said Bob Parker. "She's doing fine. You'll see a big difference in her."

"We'll take you," said Neil.

"I'm coming, too," said Sarah.

Neil opened the main door of the rescue center and beckoned Wendy Paget inside.

"Bella may be sleeping," said Emily, following behind them.

"Baa won't be," said Sarah, giggling. "He's too bouncy!"

In fact, neither of the dogs was asleep. The beagle was out of her basket and was sniffing the cocker spaniel puppy through the wire mesh that separated their pens. Little Baa's tail was wagging furiously and she whimpered with delight.

"I think Bella has really taken to Baa," said Neil. "Emily's idea to put them in pens next to each other was brilliant. Having a friend has really helped Bella's recovery."

Wendy knelt down. "Yes, she certainly looks a lot happier and more relaxed. I bet King Street is like a hotel to her considering what she's been through."

"Dad says we can take her out into the exercise field for the first time this afternoon," said Emily. "She's got a lot of her energy back now." Emily poked her fingers through the wire mesh and the beagle came toward her. She gently touched the dog's white chest and ruffled her coat. Bella was getting stronger every day.

Shortly after lunch, Neil and Emily were on their bikes and heading into Compton. "I think we should check the pet stores first," said Neil. "I don't think they'll have anything in the big shops, but there's a shabby-looking one near the library. They were selling kittens in there the other day."

"OK," Emily agreed. "Then we'll check the delis and coffee shops. I've brought a petition with me to see if we can get some signatures for the Custom Care Products boycott campaign, too."

But the visits to the pet stores revealed nothing. No one had tried to sell a litter of young beagle puppies to either of them.

"You'd be better off trying the local papers," Mr. Kemp in the High Street pet store had told them. "The new *Advertiser* comes out at lunchtime." He'd also wanted to know all about the research center. "If you leave me copies of the petition here, I'm sure a lot of my customers would sign — they're all animal lovers. I had no idea what was going on there. I thought the place was developing giant tomatoes, that sort of thing — not testing cosmetics."

As the day wore on, Neil became hotter and more discouraged. "We've visited every store owner in Compton now, except for Mrs. Smedley, but she's on the way home. We could have bought everything from coats to cockatoos — but no puppies," he groaned.

"Two lemonades please, Mrs. Smedley," said Emily, as they flopped across the counter of their local coffee shop. "And do you have the *Advertiser* yet? You keep copies here, don't you?"

Mrs. Smedley was filling a jar with candy from a large carton. She nodded and wiped her palms on her overalls. "It's just come in. You two look exhausted. What have you been up to?"

Neil explained about the beagle puppies.

"I haven't got any ads for puppies at all," the woman said. "But I'll call you if anything turns up. And you can leave some of those petitions, too. I'm sure a lot of people coming in will want to sign." Mrs. Smedley had always been a good friend to King Street Kennels.

"Thanks for the paper, Mrs. Smedley," said Neil, as they left. "We'll keep you posted about any developments."

Back at King Street Kennels, Neil and Emily found a huge plate of sandwiches on the kitchen table. There was also a note from their mother reminding them that it was Kate's birthday.

"We'd better go and give Kate her card," said Emily.

They found Kate busy cleaning out one of the pens in Kennel Block Two. Emily handed her the colored envelope and shouted, "Happy birthday!"

"Thanks, guys," she said, reading the card. "That's really thoughtful of you."

Neil slapped Kate's back, playfully. "You should be taking it easy today. I can't believe you actually showed up for work on your birthday! That's dedication to dogs for you."

Kate blushed. "I can't help it! And I'm going out with Glenn later, so I've got something to look forward to."

Neil nudged Emily in the ribs.

Kate blushed again and said something hurriedly to change the subject. "I've just looked in on Bella. She's really perking up. Sarah says you're going to take her out later."

"As soon as we've looked at this newspaper," said Neil, waving the *Advertiser* at her. "We're trying to track down the puppies. We picked up the new issue in Compton — we couldn't wait for it to arrive out here! See you later, and happy birthday!"

"Good luck," said Kate. "Hope you come up with something."

Neil and Emily spread the newspaper out on the kitchen table and eagerly scanned the classified ads.

Neil's face burst into a smile. "Listen to this!" he said. *"Beautiful beagle pups for sale. Good family pets."*

"That's it! We might have found them, Neil," said Emily, excitedly.

"You try the number, Em."

Neil listened as Emily dialed the phone. Then she nodded encouragingly to him. Someone must have answered. "Hello. I understand you have some beagle puppies for sale. Can you tell me how old they are, please?" Her face fell as she listened. "Oh, I see, um, yes. Well, no, thank you." She put the receiver down.

"What is it?" asked Neil anxiously.

Emily shook her head. "They were too young. Only two weeks old. They couldn't be the right ones."

Neil was crestfallen. "Another dead end. I can't stand much more of this!"

"At least we've found Bella's owners," said Emily.

"I suppose so." Neil looked uncertain. "It looks as if we're never going to find her puppies, though. I'm really worried — that man may just dump them if he can't find a buyer. Even if we do trace him, we might be too late."

CHAPTER EIGHT

Wednesday was another hot, humid day at King Street Kennels. The dogs were feeling the heat and an unusually quiet hush had descended over the kennel. The dogs lay stretched out in their pens and greeted Kate and Neil with quiet, grateful wags instead of the usual round of barking as they were brought fresh water.

"How's the campaign going?" Neil asked her.

"Glenn says that about thirty students are going to the rally and that they've also managed to get a lot of support from the neighborhood. There should be a good turnout on Saturday. The press will be there, too," she told Neil. "By the way, where's Sarah?" she asked as they walked over to the rescue center. "She's usually here to see Baa at this time."

"She's sort of helping Emily with a poster, I think," said Neil. "But her coloring-in isn't too hot."

Just then Sarah came running up. "Kate, Kate! Wait for me. Am I too late?"

Kate smiled. "No, here you are." She handed Sarah a bowl. "This is Baa's. Neil, can you take Bella's food for me? I'll get some water."

Sarah turned excitedly to Neil. "Baa can sit now, when I tell him. He does for his bowl, anyway. Kate showed me how."

"We'll give Bella hers first," said Neil.

The beagle was already sitting patiently when Neil opened her pen. Her short coat gleamed and looked healthy again thanks to Kate's grooming, and her large, brown eyes were bright and alert. She watched Neil put down her bowl. She waited for his command before moving. "Eat up, girl!" Neil told her. With a happy tail-wag, she moved eagerly to the bowl and began to eat.

Then Neil opened Baa's pen. The cocker spaniel was charging around and around excitedly. He began to dash backward and forward toward Sarah. "Baa, sit!" said Sarah sternly, holding up his bowl. "Baa, sit!"

Baa sat as still as he could, trembling with excitement.

Neil was impressed. "You've done really well, Squirt," he told her, taking her hand. "Come on, let's go and help Emily."

* * *

Neil spent a frustrating day on Thursday worrying about Bella. He also helped Emily add to a pile of posters in preparation for the rally. On Friday afternoon, Neil was in the rescue center after a morning spent collecting signatures for the Custom Care Products boycott petition in Compton. He was watching Bella play with Baa in her pen when Bob Parker came over with Sarah to join him. Baa wriggled away from Bella and charged back toward his own pen. Sarah picked him up and cuddled him.

Bob handed Neil the latest edition of the *Compton News.* "I thought you might like to see this. I know you've been waiting for it."

"Great!" Neil took the paper, quickly found the 'for sale' section, and scanned down the column. Moments later he closed the newspaper and handed it back. "Nothing."

Bob put a hand on Neil's shoulder. "I'm sorry, Neil. But it was a long shot, wasn't it? You might have to accept that you may never find Bella's puppies."

Neil nodded, but didn't reply.

"You and Emily have already done a great job finding Bella and making sure she's safe. Mrs. Thompson's going to be thrilled to get her dog back after all this time."

"I know." Neil watched Sarah playing with Baa and smiled.

Bob Parker nodded in Sarah's direction. "She's

very fond of him, isn't she?" he whispered. Sarah
was so involved in playing with Baa that she was not
listening to the conversation going on above her
head.

"We can't keep him, can we Dad?" said Neil.

"No. I just hope Sarah realizes that. I think I'd better have a word with her."

Neil watched as his father helped Sarah put Baa
back into his pen.

Bob took hold of Sarah's hand. "Darling," he said,
quietly. "Try not to get too attached to Baa, will you?
He'll probably have to leave us soon."

"What do you mean?" Sarah's bottom lip began to
quiver.

"Baa will probably be going to new owners. I'm
afraid we can't keep him here forever."

Sarah looked down at the spaniel puppy scrambling up at the wire mesh and trying to touch her. "But I love him," she said.

Neil swallowed hard. He knew how she must be feeling. Although he was older now, part of him still wanted to keep every dog that came into the rescue center, too.

Bob gave Sarah a hug. "I know you love him, darling. But we already have Sam. And Fudge."

Sarah started crying and ran past them both. Bob shrugged at Neil, then followed her out of the rescue center to try to calm her down.

Neil sighed. Sarah was too young to understand that they couldn't give every puppy a home themselves. Just then, he felt a wet nose push against his hand. It was Sam. "Hello, boy." Neil stroked the collie's soft ears. "How do you always seem to know when I'm feeling low?" He bent down and hugged his dog. "You know what, a walk would probably do me good. Come on, let's go."

As he turned to leave, Neil almost bumped into Emily.

"Neil!" she said. "I've been looking everywhere for you."

"What is it?" asked Neil.

"It's Mrs. Smedley," she said excitedly. "She just called. A man came into the shop and left an ad to be posted in the window. He's got some beagle puppies

for sale! She gave me the number on this card. It's a Padsham number."

A few minutes later, they were back in the house. Neil picked up the phone. Slowly, he pressed the numbers. Emily gripped the table anxiously next to him. "Is anyone there?" she whispered.

Neil shook his head. Then he nodded. Someone had answered. "Hello. Do you have some beagle puppies for sale?" he asked, trying to keep his voice calm. "Could I come and see them, please? What, now? Before six. Right. OK, we're coming. Where? Yes, I think I know. Good-bye."

Neil put the phone down. He was shaking. He turned to Emily. "I think he has Bella's puppies! They're about eight weeks old. We've got to go and see them now because he's going out soon. He lives off the main road connecting Padsham to Compton, past the Beedham turning. Come on, we've got to hurry."

Just as they grabbed their bikes, Carole Parker turned into the kennel driveway in the Range Rover. She rolled down the window. "Just a minute. Where are you going? Don't be late for dinner."

"We won't. See you, Mom," said Neil, riding away.

"We won't be long," shouted Emily, waving.

Emily looked at Neil as they waited to turn into the main road. "Where is this place? How far is it?"

"Follow me," said Neil. He knew the street. They must have ridden past it hundreds of times on their way to Padsham, but neither of them had ever been down it.

After a quarter of an hour's hard biking, they left the main road and turned into a narrow, winding lane. The farm the man had described was called Four Acres and was supposed to be just a few minutes down the street.

The main road had been busy with early evening traffic. The sudden quietness and remoteness of the street was a little unnerving, but Neil kept going. "It's not far now," he called back to Emily.

They passed a small clump of trees and then, as they turned the next bend, they saw it. A rusty, metal sign hung from a pole at the roadside. The property was bordered by a rotting picket fence, the gate was propped open, and a weed-covered driveway led to some buildings beyond. The farm seemed to consist of a cottage and a few dilapidated sheds. The yard was strewn with pieces of broken tractors.

Neil turned to Emily. "I don't like the looks of this place."

Emily shook her head. "We can't go back now."

They left their bikes by the road and walked toward the cottage. A rusty, red van, its hood open, was standing in the driveway. Neil looked at his watch. It was ten to six. They'd just made it in time.

Emily knocked on the door. A man opened it. He looked younger than he'd sounded on the phone. He was wearing overalls, and his long, dark hair hung around his unshaven face. He was wiping his hands on a dirty rag.

"We've come about the puppies, Mr. . . ." said Neil. The man didn't give him a name so Neil continued, hesitantly. "I called earlier. We got here as quickly as we could."

"Come in," the man said, glancing toward the van.

"I've been doing some work on her. I was just about to clean myself up."

Neil and Emily followed him into the small kitchen, trying not to show their unease.

"You've only just caught me. I'm on my way out, so you'll have to be quick. Wait here, I'll get him for you."

"Er, would it be possible to see the whole litter, please? How many are there?" Neil asked.

The man shook his head. "Three. But sorry, son, they're all spoken for except one. Not much point in seeing the other two."

Emily stepped forward. "What about the mother? Could we see her, please?"

The man looked at Emily. "Know a lot about dogs, do we?"

"Oh, no," said Neil quickly. "Not really. Our mom does. We're looking for a surprise present for her."

"Well, you're out of luck with the puppies' mother, I'm afraid. My friend has . . . just taken her out for a long walk. They need a lot of exercise, don't they?"

"Oh, yes," said Emily. "And grooming and everything."

"Well, do you want to see this puppy or not?"

"Yes, please," said Neil and Emily, nodding.

The man left the kitchen. Neil watched him through the window walking toward the sheds. The man paused and glanced back. Neil quickly moved out of sight. "He doesn't want us to see where they're kept," whispered Neil.

Emily nodded. "That was a lie about the long walk. And why didn't he give us his name?"

The man returned in a few minutes with a very young beagle puppy clutched in his hands. He cleared a place on the table and put it down. "There you go. He's a fine little fellow — good stock and temperament. He'll make a nice pet. Go on, pick him up," he said to Emily.

The puppy was very thin with a bulging stomach. He cowered, shivering on the table, scratching and slipping on the smooth surface with its tiny claws. Emily gently scooped him up and held him against her. She softly stroked the white markings on his forehead with her finger as the trembling puppy

nuzzled closer. "You're a sweet little thing, aren't you?" she whispered.

"He's a bit shy in here," said the man. "You should see him with the others, though. Always raring to go, that one. Well, what do you think? Do you want him?"

Neil nodded and smiled, trying not to show his concern for the puppy. "He's lovely but we haven't got any money with us. Can we come back tomorrow?"

"That'll be fine," said the man. "I want cash. Fifty dollars. Come by about this time."

Neil held out his hand. "Thank you. I'm sure he'll have a good home with us."

Reluctantly, Emily handed the puppy back to the man as he hurried them out of the door. "I'm running late. See you tomorrow."

Neil and Emily walked silently back down the drive. "Poor little thing," Emily whispered when they reached the bikes. "Did you see its stomach?"

Neil nodded. He was seething inside. "It hadn't been wormed. It's obviously not being looked after properly, poor thing. I bet they're being kept in awful conditions."

"I don't think he knows anything at all about dogs," said Emily.

"We've got to see the others, Emily. They may even be in worse shape."

Emily nodded.

"I think we should wait until he's passed us. Then we can come back and find those puppies."

Neil and Emily raced to the small clump of trees they saw earlier. They dragged their bikes off the road and crouched down. Overhead the crows were returning to roost. Their harsh cries broke the silence of the balmy evening. "We're going to be home so late," Emily whispered.

"This is more important," said Neil. "Listen, he's coming."

The red van tore past them with a trail of fumes. When it had disappeared from sight, Neil and Emily dragged their bikes back up to the road and rushed to the farm. It didn't take them long to find the puppies. As Neil peered through the broken panes of one of the small sheds, a chorus of little yaps and cries broke out.

"Quick, Emily, over here!" he cried.

As he peered into the gloom, he could make out three puppies. They were tumbling over each other to get to the door, but at least they weren't lying sick and cowering in a corner. He could see a dish of water, but the whole place looked as though it hadn't been cleaned out for days. There were empty cardboard boxes on the floor but no proper bedding.

"We've got to get them out of there," said Emily.

Neil shook his head. "We can't — we'll never get

this lock open. And we don't know for certain that they're Bella's. There's no way of proving it."

"Bella could prove it," said Emily. "The pups would come to her. They wouldn't have forgotten her."

"You're right. That's brilliant. We'll take her to-morrow before anyone's up and see how they react. I'm sure she's up to a decent walk now. Come on, let's get out of here."

CHAPTER NINE

The rest of the Parker family was sitting in the kitchen eating supper when Neil and Emily got home. "Sorry we're late, Mom," said Neil as he sidled into his place at the table. "We've had a great afternoon."

"We got lots of signatures for the petition," Emily added, without being too specific about where they'd actually gotten them from.

In fact, Carole and Bob Parker weren't about to start asking questions. They were too anxious about Sarah, who was sitting staring at her plate, refusing to eat anything.

"Come on, darling," said Carole. "You've got to eat. You've always known that we couldn't keep Baa. We've already got Sam and Fudge."

"We haven't even found a home for him yet," said Bob. "He's going to be with us a little longer, I'm sure. But you wouldn't want him to always be at the rescue center, would you? He needs a real home and he won't always be a puppy. Before long, he'll be grown up like Sam."

"Maybe you could spend a little more time with Neil and Sam," said Carole, looking at Neil. "Sam needs a lot of love from all of us, not just from Neil."

"Sure," said Neil, joining in. "And you can come to the woods and I'll show you all his favorite places. Look," he added, grinning. "Sam *wants* you to spend time with him," Sam sat up when he heard his name, and was now nuzzling up against Sarah.

"Can we go now?" asked Sarah, perking up.

"You'll have to hurry up and eat something first. It'll be your bedtime soon," said Carole, smiling her thanks at Neil.

That night Neil found it hard to fall asleep. His mind was racing as he thought about the next morning. The rally against the research center suddenly seemed less important now that they'd found the beagle pups. Neil woke before the alarm went off and silently crept into Emily's room. She was already awake and dressed. They slipped outside. Their biggest problem would be getting Bella out of her pen without disturbing the other dogs in the rescue center.

Emily slowly eased the rescue center door open just enough for Neil to squeeze through. Neil tiptoed inside, trying not to make too much noise as he made his way along the aisle toward Bella's pen. Although some of the dogs stirred to greet him, they didn't bark. Some of them looked up, yawned, and curled back up in their baskets. Baa scampered up to the fence when he saw him. Neil held his breath. An enthusiastic greeting from Baa might ruin everything. He scratched the puppy's chin through the mesh and willed him to go back to his basket. After what seemed like an eternity, the little dog sleepily padded back to his basket and curled up. Neil let out a huge sigh of relief.

Neil stepped inside Bella's pen. She was sleeping so soundly that she didn't wake up right away. "Come on, girl," he whispered to Bella as he clipped on her leash. "We're going to find your puppies."

A minute later, Neil emerged from the rescue center holding Bella's leash.

"What took you so long?" whispered Emily.

"Puppy problems," said Neil.

They crossed the exercise field and slipped out into the fields beyond. The ground was wet with early-morning dew, and a white floating mist stretched as far as they could see.

"You *are* sure about this path, aren't you?" asked Emily suspiciously.

Neil nodded. "We just go as far as the woods and

then follow the path that runs along that small stream. And then it's straight across the fields again. I've brought the map." They'd found a path on the map, which led from the woods near King Street Kennels to the street where the farm was. It cut off quite a bit of the trip and would be better for Bella than trudging down the main road.

"Bella's enjoying it," said Emily. The beagle looked up and wagged her tail when she heard her name. She'd kept her nose to the ground all the way. She behaved well on the leash, keeping to heel and not straining, but Neil sensed that she longed to be running free.

At last, they reached the road. "We turn right now," said Neil, looking at the map. "Just a little way along and Four Acres should be on our left."

"I hope that man isn't up yet," said Emily.

"We'll have to hope he's sleeping late," said Neil.

They walked quickly along the road. Suddenly, as they rounded a bend, the familiar run-down sheds appeared in front of them. They stopped for a moment to catch their breath. Neil knelt down and ruffled Bella's ears. "Are you ready for this, girl?" She looked up at him eagerly.

Emily smiled. "She's all right."

As they drew nearer to the driveway, Bella seemed to hesitate. Then she began to sniff the ground in a more urgent way.

"What is it, Bella?" whispered Neil.

"I think she recognizes the place," said Emily.
"Should we let her off her leash?"

"I suppose so. We need to see what she does."

"I don't think she'll go far," said Neil, slipping off her leash.

The beagle seemed to hang back for a moment. Then as they turned into the gateway, she suddenly darted forward with her nose to the ground.

"Here, girl!" called Neil in dismay as the beagle sped away from them, down the driveway.

"Oh, no!" Emily whispered.

"Look at that!" cried Neil. "Straight there! She's going to those sheds. There's *no way* this is the first time she's been to this place."

"We've got to get her back," said Emily. "Before she wakes the puppies."

As they ran along, Neil kept glancing upward, hoping that the man didn't appear in the window of the house. Bella reached the shed door. She was scratching and whining. The puppies were awake now. Their tiny yelps seemed terribly loud in the still morning.

"Bella. Here!" called Neil. As he ran forward with her leash, the door of the cottage opened.

The man stood there in his bathrobe, blearily rubbing his eyes. "What the . . . ?" he began. He caught sight of Neil and Bella.

"Quickly!" screamed Emily.

Neil put the leash on Bella and dragged her away.

He began to run and he didn't look back. Emily was running, too.

"Stop! You . . ." They heard the man's voice bellowing after them. "What are you up to? Come back here!"

Neil and Emily kept running, down the road toward the footpath, praying that the man wouldn't follow them. As they stumbled across the field, Neil thought it was a good thing they'd taken this route. On the road they'd have stood no chance — the man would easily have caught up with them in his car.

They didn't stop until they reached the woods. Emily glanced back. "It's all right. He's not coming. He hasn't followed us."

They stood still for a minute, trying to get their breath back. "He must have seen Bella and recognized us," said Neil. "He'll know we're on to him."

"We'll have to tell Mom and Dad," said Emily.

Neil nodded. "You know what this means — he'll get rid of them now for sure, as quickly as he can. The puppies are the only thing linking him to Bella — he can't risk that. He'd be in trouble for stealing a dog. He'll have to dump them right away. Anywhere. Possibly even the river . . . we've got to stop him!"

CHAPTER TEN

It was nearly nine o'clock by the time Neil and Emily got home. They'd already been missed, but there was no time for recriminations. Once Bob and Carole had heard what Neil and Emily had to say about the beagle pups, they sprang into action. Carole called the police while Bob put Bella safely back in the rescue center. He told Neil and Emily to wait in the car for him.

Minutes later, Bob Parker was beside them. "The police are going to get there as quickly as they can," he said. "But most of their men are busy at the rally."

"We've got to get over there, Dad," urged Neil. "We need to watch the place in case the man gets rid of the puppies before they arrive. He'll want to destroy the evidence."

Bob jumped into the car and pulled out of the drive-way onto the road.

"Take a left toward Padsham," shouted Emily from the backseat. "And then it's another left turn before Beedham. We'll show you. Watch out for the tight corners, though!"

Bob gripped the steering wheel, staring ahead. "Can you see the place from the road?" he asked, as they sped along the narrow country streets.

"Yes," said Neil. "But he'll be able to see us, too."

"OK, I'll drive right past. You two look out and see if there's any sign of him."

"I'll check if his van's there," said Neil.

Bob slowed down as they passed the run-down farm. Neil and Emily strained to look out of the window.

"He's there!" screamed Emily. "And he's carrying a large box to the van. It must be the puppies!"

"We're too late, Dad!" Neil shouted. "You've got to turn around."

Bob quickly pulled over to the side of the road. "This street's too narrow for us to turn around. Keep watching him. We don't know which way he's going to go yet."

"He's put the box in the van and now he's getting in," said Neil, urgently. "That box looked very small. The puppies will be crushed."

"Do something!" pleaded Emily.

Bob threw the Range Rover into reverse. "I'll try and block him," he shouted.

It was too late. The red van shot out of the driveway and sped toward the main road.

"He must know we're after him. Don't worry, we won't let him get away. Hold on!" Bob told them as he pulled into the driveway and took off after the van.

For a time, they lost sight of the van completely as they raced down the twisting road. "He's vanished!" said Neil, desperately.

"It's just these bends," said Bob. "He can't be far ahead. We'll see him when the road straightens out. Here, catch this." He tossed the cell phone to Neil. "Call Sergeant Moorhead. Tell him what's happening."

"We don't know which way he's gone," cried Emily, as they reached the main road.

Bob craned forward over the wheel. "There," he shouted, catching sight of a speck of red up ahead. "He's heading for the Padsham town center."

Neil watched the road as Emily made a frantic call to the police on the phone. He was thinking about the puppies being tossed around in the cardboard box in the back of the van. "I'll kill him," he muttered. "If those puppies are hurt, I'll . . ."

A moment later a police car with its siren wailing tore past them on the other side of the road.

"Oh, no!" cried Neil. "They're going the wrong way!"

"Look," shouted Emily suddenly, pointing at the van — which seemed to be getting closer. "We're gaining on him. He's slowing down!"

"There's something happening up ahead," said Bob.

"There are people there in the road. Look!" Neil shouted. "It's the rally! Excellent!"

"They've blocked the main road," said Bob.

Ahead of the Range Rover, the red van had screeched to a stop. Several people with banners taking part in the rally had spilled out from the research center driveway onto the main road. The crowd was a lot bigger than either Neil or Emily had expected. There were several policemen at the periphery of the crowd trying to move them off the road. A TV news camera crew was recording the chanting of slogans near the main gate.

The Range Rover pulled up a couple of yards behind the van. Bob smiled. "We've got him now!"

"Look, Dad!" Neil warned. "He's trying to turn around. He's going to come back on the other side."

The red van backed onto the grass, crashing into the UNIVERSAL LABORATORIES sign. The van began to spin its wheels, revving its engine ready to surge away.

Bob saw his chance. "Hold on," he shouted to Neil and Emily. He quickly swung the Range Rover in front of the van, blocking its escape.

For a second, the man in the red van seemed to

hesitate, unsure what to do next. They were so close they could see his grim face scowling at them.

Suddenly, the crowd seemed to push forward toward them.

"Look," said Emily. "There's Kate and Glenn."

Neil felt his heart racing, but there was no time to be scared. He leaped from the car and shouted across to Glenn. "It's him! The man who stole the puppies! Stop him!"

The man had jumped down from the van. He swayed like a frightened rabbit, wondering which way to bolt, and then headed toward the open fields. Glenn broke from the crowd and raced after him, followed by a policeman and Kate.

Bob Parker clambered out of the Range Rover over the passenger seat — his own door was blocked by the van. "Stay here!" he shouted to Neil and Emily, as he joined in the chase. "Get the puppies."

Neil and Emily watched as Glenn threw himself at the fleeing man and brought him down to the ground roughly.

They ran together to the back of the red van, but the doors wouldn't open. They were jammed tight against the broken signpost. Neil pulled at the broken post and sign. "They're trapped!"

People from the crowd came forward.

"We've got to get the puppies out of there!" Emily shouted. "They might be hurt! They'll suffocate in this heat."

Suddenly, Neil felt an arm on his shoulder. "Let me help."

Neil turned around. It was Mr. Pritchard, the man from Universal Laboratories. As Mr. Pritchard and a few students from the crowd struggled to free the van's doors, the camera crew closed in on them to record the incident.

Finally, Neil wrenched open the back doors. A sealed cardboard box lay on its side where it had fallen over during the bumpy journey. Neil and Emily could hear scratching and whimpering.

Emily began to pull away the heavy packing tape that sealed the box closed. "They must be terrified!" she cried.

"They'd better not be hurt," muttered Neil.

Emily's fingers were trembling. From inside the box, the yelping and scratching grew louder. At last, she tore open the lid. Three small beagle pups leaped up at the sides, scrabbling to get out.

"Are they all right?" asked Emily, anxiously.

"I think so," whispered Neil. He put his hand into the box. Little wet noses and tongues snuffled and grabbed at his fingers. He could hardly believe it. They had done it. They had rescued the puppies! It was all over. Gently, he lifted out one of the struggling, yapping bundles and passed it to Emily.

"Oh, you're beautiful," gasped Emily, as she held the soft, short-haired beagle puppy on her knee. The

little pup licked her hand and buried its white muzzle into her T-shirt.

The crowd broke into applause.

Kate appeared at Neil's side and patted him on the back. "Wow!" she said, laughing. "What an entrance! I thought you weren't going to make it to the rally when I didn't see you earlier."

Neil wiped his brow. "We were . . . held up!" He lifted another brown-and-white bundle onto his knee. Big, brown eyes stared up at him. A long thin tail wagged. "You're OK, little fella," he said, as the puppy began to chew his finger. "You're safe now."

That afternoon, three washed and gleaming puppies were reunited with Bella in her pen at King Street

Kennels. It was a very special moment and Neil and Emily were really choked up as they watched Bella greet the tumbling playful pups. She sniffed and washed each one in turn, glancing up from time to time.

Carole, Sarah, Bob, and Mike Turner all looked on anxiously.

"She looks so happy," whispered Emily.

Bella then retreated to her basket and sat watching as the puppies tumbled and jostled around her.

"She seems very proud of them," said Neil.

"Whoops!" laughed Sarah, as one of the puppies rolled against its mother, only to find itself held down by a firm paw and given another good washing.

"Are they going to be all right, Mike?" asked Emily.

"They've been kept in pretty poor conditions. One has an ear infection, another a sore eye. I'll leave some drops and ointment. They all need worming right away, but once they're cleaned up and are given the right food, they should be fine."

"We're hoping to hear from the owners tomorrow," said Bob.

"Yes, they'll need to get their own vet to look at them again in a few days."

After several minutes, Bella's puppies grew tired and one by one they flopped down beside their mother. Soon they were all breathing in unison — their eyes tightly closed and their little brown-and-

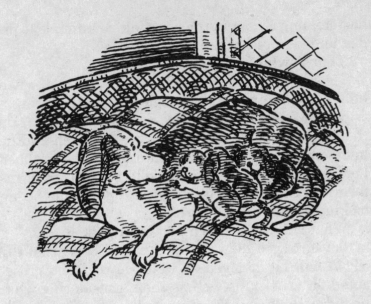

white bodies heaving gently. With a final contented lick and a sniff, Bella sighed and closed her eyes, too.

Neil smiled and turned to Emily. "We did it, Em, didn't we? We did it!"

"What happened to the man who stole Bella?" asked Mike, as he packed his bag.

"Sergeant Moorhead called just before you arrived," said Bob. "The man confessed."

"Of course, he did!" said Neil angrily.

"He was a salesman dealing in second-hand agricultural machine parts who often traveled all over the country. It seems it wasn't the first time he'd done this sort of thing. He'd been involved with a

dog-stealing racket in the past, taking animals to or-
der, and he already had one conviction."

"That's awful," gasped Emily.

"He saw another chance for some easy cash when
he noticed the pregnant beagle in a park during a
trip to Middlesbrough. He couldn't resist it. He
thought that beagles were used in research and he
knew about Universal Laboratories, so he grabbed
her. Unfortunately for him, Bella escaped from his
farm. He thought he might get caught so he began
looking for a quick, cheap sale."

"What will happen to him?" Emily asked.

Bob shrugged. "I'm not sure, but it seems that the
SPCA will be involved as well. He could be prose-
cuted for cruelty, as well as theft, considering what
he did to Bella and the state he kept the puppies in.
Hopefully, he'll be banned from ever keeping
animals."

That evening, Glenn and Kate arrived with news of
the rally, and Wendy Paget came with them. The
protest had generated a lot of local support and me-
dia attention.

"There should be plenty of pictures in the papers
tomorrow," said Kate. "The TV report has already
been aired. There were some great shots of Glenn
holding up a sign and shouting!"

"He was better at catching the beagle thief," said

Neil. "Did you see how quickly he caught and tackled him?"

Glenn reddened and laughed. "I've just got long legs, that's all!"

Kate hugged him. "You were great!"

"It looks as though the rally did a lot of good all around," said Glenn. "Word is coming through that Custom Care Products *is* going to cancel their contract with Universal Laboratories. They're going to stop this type of testing on animals. All the bad publicity is affecting their reputation."

"That's great news," said Bob.

"I don't think it's going to be long before the government bans cosmetics testing on animals altogether," said Glenn.

"You've done well, too," Kate said to Neil and Emily.

"Yes, Bella looks so contented. Her puppies are adorable," added Glenn.

"They're really sweet," said Sarah. "Nearly as nice as Baa."

Wendy Paget suddenly looked at Bob and smiled.

"We've got some news for you, sweetheart," said Bob. He paused. "We've found a home for Baa."

As Sarah's face began to crumple, he took her onto his knee. "No, listen, it couldn't be better. Wendy's going to look after him. Baa is going to live with Wendy and Glenn. They've been wanting a puppy for ages."

Wendy knelt down next to them. "I want you to promise to come visit us every week," she said. "You'll always be Baa's special friend. We'll be bringing him to your dad's classes when he's old enough, so you'll see him then, too."

Sarah was quiet for a minute. "Can I come to visit twice a week?"

"Sarah!" said Carole, and everyone laughed.

"You can come as often as you want!" said Wendy.

The expected phone call about Bella came from Joan Thompson the next morning. She was overjoyed to hear that Bella and her puppies were safe and would drive over from Middlesbrough right away. She was desperate to see Bella again.

A large, fancy car pulled up at the kennel shortly before six o'clock. Joan Thompson was close to tears as she got out of the car. Dressed in a green jacket and blue jeans, she flicked loose strands of graying hair out of her eyes. Her face lit up when she saw Bella, who was waiting with Emily. The beagle tore across the yard toward her and leaped into her owner's arms.

Neil and Emily stood watching them together, feeling quite moved. Sam sat at their side. Neil ruffled the collie's ears. "What if we lost you, Sam?" He couldn't even bear to think of it.

Mrs. Thompson turned to Bob Parker. "I don't know how to begin to thank you."

"Don't thank me," said Bob. "It's Neil and Emily who masterminded their great escape."

Mrs. Thompson smiled at them. "I hardly know what to say. It's wonderful what you've done." She turned back to Bob. "I've brought the reward with me of course, but please let me know what I owe you for the kennel fee."

Bob shook his head. "That's all right, there's no charge. Bella was kept in the rescue center."

"Then please let me make a donation. It's the least I can do," said Mrs. Thompson, as Carole Parker showed her into the office.

Carole returned a couple of minutes later with a wide grin on her face. "Hey, you two! There's something here you should see." She was holding up a check.

Emily stared at the amount and then handed it over to Neil. "Wow! It's enormous!"

Neil punched the air. "I think we'll be able to get that modem and scanner after all!" he said. "King Street Kennels will be online at last! World Wide Web here we come!"